W9-BEK-580

F

S

*A portion of the author's royalties from this
book will go to Libearty, the world campaign
for the protection of bears.*

Text copyright © 1994 by Frances Thomas
Illustrations copyright © 1994 by Ruth Brown
CIP Data is available.
First published in the United States 1995 by
Dutton Children's Books,
a division of Penguin Books USA Inc.
375 Hudson Street, New York, New York 10014
Originally published in Great Britain 1994 by
Andersen Press Ltd., London
Typography by Carolyn Boschi
Printed in Italy
First American Edition
ISBN 0-525-45362-8
1 3 5 7 9 10 8 6 4 2

The Bear & Mr. Bear

by Frances Thomas

pictures by Ruth Brown

DUTTON CHILDREN'S BOOKS
New York

Although he must have had another name—a real name—everyone in the village called him Mr. Bear. Grumpy and cross, shaggy and unsmiling, the old man never spoke a word more than necessary. In the streets, children stuck out their tongues behind his back. He didn't seem to notice.

Once, long ago, Mr. Bear had been as friendly as anybody else. But sad things had happened to him, and he had forgotten how to be happy.

For many years, the old man had lived all alone in a big house on the hill. Behind the house was a large garden and, around it, a high wall. Inside the house, Mr. Bear grew older and crosser.

One day Mr. Bear had to do an errand in town. He meant to come and go as quickly as he could, but it was a carnival day and the crowds of people pushed him this way and that. Soon he found himself in the town square, where there were jugglers and candy sellers and even a noisy carousel.

At the carnival was a red-haired man who held a stick and a chain. At the end of the chain was a bear with a ring through his nose and shackles on his back paws. A muzzle kept his mouth shut. The bear was smelly, and his coat was matted. His eyes were dull and runny.

When the trainer poked him with a stick, the bear stood
on his hind legs. The man poked again, and the bear
jumped, faster and faster, lumbering from one foot to the
other. He appeared to be dancing, and all the people
laughed and clapped.

But Mr. Bear saw that the bear did not dance for joy. He looked hard at the bear, but the bear looked right past him with sad, dull eyes.

"Dance!" shouted the red-haired man. The bear danced, and the people clapped.

Mr. Bear pushed his way through the crowds, looking neither left nor right. "Cross as a bear," the people muttered as he passed. He left the square and the town and went slowly up the hill to his big house.

That night, Mr. Bear could not sleep. He did not think of the jugglers or the carousel, but he remembered the bear with the sad, dull eyes.

Then he sat up in bed. His brow was furrowed. He suddenly had an idea.

Very early the next morning, Mr. Bear readied his horse and wagon and set off for town. Almost no one was in the streets, except the sweeper and the baker, who was yawning as he opened his shop. The wagons and the tents, the candy sellers and the carousel were all gone.

Mr. Bear saw a young girl carrying water.

"Which way did the carnival go?" he asked.

"That way," she replied, pointing.

Mr. Bear did not thank her. He clucked his tongue to his horses, and the wagon pulled away.

Cross as a bear, the little girl thought. She shook her head.

Mr. Bear left town. The sun rose in the sky, and the road was wide and dusty. At midday, he found what he was looking for. The red-haired man was sitting by the side of the road and eating a sausage. The man's horse was eating grass. And there in a cage slumped the dirty old bear, eating nothing at all.

"I've come to buy your bear," said Mr. Bear. The man laughed and took another bite of sausage. Mr. Bear took out his purse and showed one gold piece.

"The bear's not for sale," said the man. Mr. Bear showed him another gold piece. And another. Finally the man yawned.

"Oh, well. I've had enough of bears anyway. They're too cross. I'll stick to juggling in the future."

The man took the gold pieces, and he and Mr. Bear lifted the creaking wooden cage onto the wagon. The bear growled. Mr. Bear took some apples from his bag and fed them to the bear.

The journey home was long and bumpy. Whenever the bear would growl, Mr. Bear would give him an apple. In this way they made their way home, though by the time they got there it was nearly dark.

That night, the bear slept soundly in Mr. Bear's woods. Mr. Bear had given him a sleeping potion, mixed in a bowl of water. While the bear slept, Mr. Bear removed the shackles and the muzzle. He took off the chain. He chopped up the cage and burned it.

Meanwhile, the bear dreamed. He dreamed of times long ago, of playing in the hills with his mother, his sisters and brothers. The bear dreamed of splashing in a silvery stream and catching a fish. He dreamed of rolling in soft grass and sniffing for ripe berries.

Then he dreamed of how the hunters had come with their guns. They had shot his mother and had taken all the cubs to a town and sold them.

When the bear remembered this, he woke with an angry growl. Then he opened his mouth wide and yawned. He lifted up his head and stretched. There was no chain to jerk him back to the ground and no cold, slippery cage—only soft, sweet grass. The bear stood up unsteadily. He could smell the delicious scent of fresh water.

The bear took one step, then another. Still no chain jerked his head. Nobody shouted or waved a stick. Into the stream he lumbered, slowly at first, then plunging in right up to his shoulders. Cold water ran over his dry, matted fur and down his burning throat.

When the bear shook himself all over, he remembered how hungry he was. Across the garden, sitting quietly on the grass, was the man who had given him some apples.

Now there was more food: honeycomb and nuts, fresh fish and berries. The bear ate everything. He had not eaten such good food for a long time and was beginning—just beginning—not to feel cross or frightened.

The bear looked at Mr. Bear, who looked back.

Mr. Bear smiled.